BOOK 5a

The Ladybird Key Words Reading Scheme

KT-172-158

Where we go

by W. MURRAY

with illustrations
by MARTIN AITCHISON

Ladybird Books Ltd Loughborough

Jane, Peter, Mummy and Daddy all want to go for a walk.

"We will go up the hill," says Daddy. "Yes," says Peter, "let us go up the hill. It is fun up there."

Pat the dog wants to go. He jumps up and down. "Yes," says Peter to Pat, "you can come. You can come for a walk with us. You can come up the hill."

"No," says Jane to her cat. "You cannot come for a walk. You will be at home. You can have some milk."

"Come on," says Daddy. "Off we go. Off we go up the hill."

---

new words   walk   hill

Off they go. Peter walks with Daddy, and Jane walks with Mummy. They go by the house and the shops. They see some cars and a bus. On they go to the hill.

"I like to go where there are trees and flowers," says Jane. "Where do you want to go, Peter?"

"I want to go where I can see rabbits and horses. I like to go by the farm," says Peter.

Daddy says, "Yes, we can go by the farm."

"Look," says Jane, "I can read where it says TO THE HILL."

"Yes," says Peter, "and I can read BUS STOP."

new words   by   where

Now they walk by the water. Pat wants to go into the water. Peter will not let him. "I want to look for fish," he says.

"I can see two down there," says Jane. "Look, Peter, can you see a big one and a little one?"

"Where?" says Peter. Then he says, "Yes, I can see them. I can see them now."

Mummy and Daddy go on. They are by the trees. "I can see the hill now," says Mummy. Daddy looks for the children. "Come on," he says. "We will go on to the farm. We can get some milk there."

"Yes," says Mummy, "we will all have some milk."

---

new words   now   them

Mummy, Daddy and the children walk up to the farm. They go by the pigs. There are two big pigs and two little ones.

Jane likes the little pigs. She gives them some of her cake. Peter has some apples and he gives some of them to one of the big pigs. "This big pig likes apples," he says. "He wants all of them now."

"Where are Mummy and Daddy?" says Jane.

"They are by the cows," says Peter. "They want to get some milk for us. Come on, Jane, and have some milk now."

The two children walk to Mummy and Daddy. They want some milk.

new words

pigs   of

They all go in. "Here you are," says the man, "here is some milk for you." Jane and Peter and Mummy have some of the milk, and Daddy says, "Now I want some, please."

The man works on the farm and he likes to talk to them about it. He talks about the cows, and he talks about the pigs. He likes his work.

Then Daddy talks to the man about the walk. He says where they want to go. "Yes," says the man, "I like to walk up the hill. I like to be up there. You can see the sea."

He gives Pat some milk.

---

new words   talk   about

They can see the top now. They can see the top of the hill.

"We will stop at the top to eat," says Daddy. "Yes," says Peter, "let us walk to the top and then eat. We all want to eat."

"Look," says Jane, "I can see DANGER." "Yes," says Daddy, "do not go there."

Mummy says "Can you see the train?" "Yes," says Jane, "I can see it down there. It looks like a toy train."

"Look at the little houses," says Peter. "It is fun to see them like this. Now I can see the farm." The children talk about the farm.

---

new words   top   eat

Here they are in the sun at th
top of the hill. Mummy, Daddy an
the children all like the sun. The
stop now to look down the hill.

They can see the farm and
man with some cows. The cows ar
going to the water by the trees. A
little red car is going to the farm
The train is going to the station.

" Look," says Jane, " I can see th
sea. I can see the sun on the sea."

" Yes," says Peter, " I can see it
I can see the sea. There is a boa
on it."

The children like to talk abou
the sea.

---

new words   sun   going

There are trees at the top of th
hill. Daddy says, " Now we will ea
by this tree." Jane and Peter hel
Mummy, and then they all sit dow
to eat.

Daddy wants to sit by the tree
Mummy and the children like to b
in the sun. Pat sits with them. The
all sit where they can look dow
the hill.

Daddy talks about the afternoor
He says, "We are going to play in th
sun this afternoon, and then we ar
going to walk down the hill for tea.

" Good," says Peter, " it will b
fun to play with Daddy th
afternoon."

---

new words   sit   afternoon

It is the afternoon. Daddy,
Mummy, Jane and Peter sit in the
sun at the top of the hill. Pat wants
to eat. The children talk about the
games they like.

Then Peter says to Daddy, "Are
you going to play with us this
afternoon? You said so." "Yes,"
says Jane, "you said so."

"Yes," says Daddy, "I said it, so
I will play. What do you want to
play?"

"Let us play with the ball," says
Peter. Jane says, "Yes, that will be
good fun."

Daddy and Jane have the ball.
Peter wants to get it, and Daddy
and Jane have to stop him.

---

new words   said   so

Now they are all going down the hill. Mummy says, "I like to sit in the sun for the afternoon."

Pat runs on. "What can the dog see?" says Daddy. "He can see rabbits," says Peter. They all look at the dog.

"Yes, they are rabbits," say Peter. "I said so. Look, he is going after them."

"Run after him, Peter," say Mummy. "Get him, Jane."

Pat runs after the rabbits, and Peter runs after Pat. Jane says, "Stop, Pat. Come here. Be a good dog and come here." Pat runs on. Peter cannot get him.

Then the rabbits go down. Pat cannot get at them now.

---

new words

run after

Down go the rabbits, so that the dog cannot get them. Pat wants to go down after them.

" Look, he is going down after the rabbits now," says Jane. " Pull him out, Peter. Pull him out, please." " Yes," says Mummy, " pull him out now, Peter."

Peter pulls and pulls at Pat. " Here he comes," says Jane. "Good for you, Peter."

Now Pat is out. He runs away. " Let him go," says Daddy, " he will come after us. We have to go on now."

The afternoon sun is going down. Mummy says she wants some tea. They walk on down the hill. Pat comes after them.

---

new words   pull   out

The children talk about the dog and the rabbits. "It was good of you to pull Pat out," says Jane to Peter.

"I must have some tea after that," says Peter. "Yes, we are going to have some tea now," says Jane, "Daddy said so."

Here they are at a tea shop. "It says AFTERNOON TEAS," says Jane. "I can read it."

"Let us go in and sit down out of the sun," says Peter. "I want to eat." "Yes," says Mummy, "we can eat here, but what about the dog?"

"He can come in," says Daddy, "but he must be a good dog."

"Yes," says Jane to Pat. "You must be a good dog."

---

new words   must   but

In they go. "You must be a good dog," says Jane to Pat. "You must sit here by my chair and not run about."

Daddy pulls out a chair for Mummy. Peter sits on a little chair, and Daddy has a big chair.

"What are we going to eat?" asks Daddy. "I must have some tea, but I do not want to eat," says Mummy.

"Can I have some cake, please?" asks Peter. "Can I have some milk, please?" asks Jane.

The girl comes up to them, and Daddy asks her for tea and milk and cakes. After this they all talk about the afternoon. "It was a good game at the top of the hill," says Peter.

---

new words   chair   asks

After they have had tea Jane and Peter see a boy and a girl come into the tea shop. "Look," says Jane, "they go to our school. We must talk to them."

"Can we talk to them now please?" Peter asks Daddy. "Yes," he says, "but let Pat sit here by my chair."

Jane and Peter go to talk to the boy and girl. They pull out chairs and sit down. "We have had our tea," says Peter.

They talk about the afternoon walk to the top of the hill. Then they talk about school.

Pat runs to Jane. "No, Pat," she says, "you are not going to run about in here. Daddy said so."

---

new words   had   our

Daddy gets up from his chair.
" We have had our tea and now we
must go," he says. "We will walk
to the station and go home by
train." The children like this.

They go out from the shop and
walk down the street. In the street
the children look in the sweet shops
and the toy shops, but they do not
stop. Pat pulls Jane after him.

Peter asks Daddy where the
station is. "It is in this street," says
Daddy. "On you go, and do not let
the dog run away from you."

The children want to get to the
station. They like to go by train.

---

new words   from   street

The children soon come to the station. They go in from the street.

As they go in, a big train pulls out from the station. They look as it is going by.

"It is a goods train," says Peter, "and there are pigs and cows on it."

Pat wants to run after it, but Jane will not let him. "Keep by me," she says to her dog, "you must not run after the train."

As Mummy and Daddy come up, Jane asks, "Where is our train?" "It will be here soon," says Daddy, "the man said so."

Then the train comes in. "Come on," says Mummy, "let us get in. We will soon be home."

---

new words   soon   as

As soon as they sit down in the train the children look out of the window. From the window they can see more and more streets and houses going by.

" Now we can see the hill where we had our walk," says Jane. "Look out of the window, Mummy, you can see more now. You can see the top of the hill. I can see where we had our game."

" Can you see the farm, Jane?" asks Peter. " Yes," she says, "there are some cows by the farm house and some more cows by the pigs."

" Now I can see where you had to pull Pat away from the rabbits," she says.

---

new words   window   more

Who is the other man in th
train? He is from the farm, and h
talks to Daddy about it.

Who is the girl with Jane? Th
man from the farm is her Daddy.

Who is the other boy? He i
from Peter's school. He eats a
apple. He has some more apple
and gives one to Jane, one to Peter
and one to the other girl.

Jane and Peter talk to the bo
and girl about the walk they hav
had. The girl asks Jane to come t
tea at the farm.

As Daddy looks out of the windov
he says, "We will soon come to ou
station."

new words

who   other

As the train stops, Peter look out of the window. " Which statio is this ?" he asks. "Yes, which is it? asks Jane.

"It is our station," says Dadd "We get out here. Get the bag Which are our bags?"

Mummy gets her bag. Daddy ha the other. Then they all get out.

Jane talks to the other girl, wh helps her with Pat. " Thank you, she says.

They go from the station to th street as soon as they can. " Pa wants to walk," says Jane. " Yes, says Mummy, " but we must get bus."

" Let us sit on top of the bus, says Peter.

new words

which bag

They walk down the street
"Which is our bus?" asks Peter
"Which is it?" he asks again. "No
this one, the other one," say
Mummy. She asks Peter to take th
dog into the bus.

But Pat will not get on. He want
to run away.

"You must get on," says Peter
"Here comes Daddy," says Jane
from the window, "he will help."

Daddy helps Mummy on to th
bus. Then Peter takes the bag from
Daddy, as Daddy puts Pat on to
the bus.

More boys who go to Peter'
school get on. They talk to Pete
about the game they have had.

---

new words   again   takes

Jane and her brother are goin
down the street in the bus.

"Which bag has the sweets?
asks Jane, who wants to eat agair
"The other one," says Mummy. A
Jane takes out the apples she give
her brother one. "You can hav
some more," she says.

Soon the bus stops by the Fir
Station. Peter looks out of th
window. "There is the Fire Station,"
he says. "I can see the men. Look
There go the firemen!" he say
"There must be a fire."

"Where there is fire there i
danger," says Mummy. "I do no
like it."

"The men will soon put out th
fire," says Daddy.

---

new words

brother   men

Peter and his sister get off th
bus to walk home. Soon they go b
the school. "What do you like t
do at school?" Jane asks he
brother. "I like to read and draw,
says Peter. "So do I," says his sister
"or I like to make things," she says

"Look, Daddy is going to tal
to that policeman," Peter says
"Yes," says Jane, "we know him
and we know his little boy wh
comes to our school."

Mummy talks to the men in th
shop. She wants some things for th
house. Peter takes the bags agai
to help Mummy. He and his siste
want to go home now.

new words   sister   know

"Look," says Peter to his sister. "what is this?"

"Read all about it!" says the man. "Read all about it!"

Peter knows how to read. He reads "BIG FIRE THIS AFTERNOON."

"We saw the firemen go," says Jane to her brother. "We saw them from the bus. The men know how to put a fire out. They will have put it out by now."

Peter says to his sister, "I can read some more. Look, it says DANGER, MEN AT WORK." He reads it again to his Daddy, and Jane reads to her Mummy.

Daddy says "It is good that our children know how to read."

new words

how   saw

The two children are at home with Mummy and Daddy. Jane and Peter know they will soon have to go to bed.

"We saw how to milk cows," says Jane. "Yes," says Peter to his sister, "and we saw how the rabbits can jump. The man at the farm said we can go up there again. I want to see the horses again."

"The girl at the farm will soon ask us up to tea," says Jane to her brother. "Daddy will take us up by car. Then we can have fun."

"Come on," says Mummy, "I have to take you off to bed now. Up we go."

---

no new words

New words used in this book

Total number of new words 46

THE LOW COUNTRIES

Hanover •

WESTPHALIA

Rembrandt
Birthplace: Leyden
place of work: Amsterdam

GERMANY

• Cologne

Siegen •

ege

A Ladybird Book
Series 701

When one knows something of the background to the lives and characters of the great artists, and how their work was influenced by their environment, the pleasure of a visit to an art gallery can be greatly enhanced.

This book tells of the lives of Rubens, Rembrandt and Vermeer, and a number of the superb full-colour illustrations show them actually at work on great masterpieces. It is a book which will fascinate children— and many adults.

Artists in this book:

RUBENS (1577-1640)

REMBRANDT (1606-1669)

VERMEER (1632-1675)